Dear Parents and Educators,

Welcome to Penguin Young Readers! A: know that each child develops at his or her own pace—in terms of speech, critical thinking, and, of course, reading. Penguin Young Readers recognizes this fact. As a result, each Penguin Young Readers book is assigned a traditional easy-to-read level (1–4) as well as a Guided Reading Level (A–P). Both of these systems will help you choose the right book for your child. Please refer to the back of each book for specific leveling information. Penguin Young Readers features esteemed authors and illustrators, stories about favorite characters, fascinating nonfiction, and more!

Strawberry Shortcake™
We Love You, Strawberry Shortcake!

LEVEL **2**

GUIDED READING LEVEL **G**

This book is perfect for a **Progressing Reader** who:
- can figure out unknown words by using picture and context clues;
- can recognize beginning, middle, and ending sounds;
- can make and confirm predictions about what will happen in the text; and
- can distinguish between fiction and nonfiction.

Here are some **activities** you can do during and after reading this book:
- Compare/Contrast: Orange Blossom's gift for Strawberry Shortcake is not like the other gifts. How is her gift different? How is her gift the same as the other gifts Strawberry receives?
- Make Connections: If you were invited to Strawberry Shortcake's party, what gift would you bring? What would make your gift special? How would your gift show Strawberry how much you love her?

Remember, sharing the love of reading with a child is the best gift you can give!

—Bonnie Bader, EdM
    Penguin Young Readers program

*Penguin Young Readers are leveled by independent reviewers applying the standards developed by Irene Fountas and Gay Su Pinnell in *Matching Books to Readers: Using Leveled Books in Guided Reading*, Heinemann, 1999.

Penguin Young Readers
Published by the Penguin Group
Penguin Group (USA) Inc., 375 Hudson Street, New York, New York 10014, USA
Penguin Group (Canada), 90 Eglinton Avenue East, Suite 700,
Toronto, Ontario M4P 2Y3, Canada
(a division of Pearson Penguin Canada Inc.)
Penguin Books Ltd., 80 Strand, London WC2R 0RL, England
Penguin Group Ireland, 25 St. Stephen's Green, Dublin 2, Ireland
(a division of Penguin Books Ltd.)
Penguin Group (Australia), 250 Camberwell Road,
Camberwell, Victoria 3124, Australia
(a division of Pearson Australia Group Pty. Ltd.)
Penguin Books India Pvt. Ltd., 11 Community Centre, Panchsheel Park,
New Delhi—110 017, India
Penguin Group (NZ), 67 Apollo Drive, Rosedale, Auckland 0632, New Zealand
(a division of Pearson New Zealand Ltd.)
Penguin Books (South Africa) (Pty.) Ltd., 24 Sturdee Avenue,
Rosebank, Johannesburg 2196, South Africa

Penguin Books Ltd., Registered Offices:
80 Strand, London WC2R 0RL, England

Strawberry Shortcake™ and related trademarks © 2011 Those Characters From Cleveland, Inc. Used
under license by Penguin Young Readers Group. American Greetings with rose logo is a trademark
of AGC, LLC. First published in 2009 by Grosset & Dunlap, an imprint of Penguin Group (USA) Inc.
Published in 2011 by Penguin Young Readers, an imprint of Penguin Group (USA) Inc.,
345 Hudson Street, New York, New York 10014. Printed in the U.S.A.

Library of Congress Control Number: 2009009296

ISBN 978-0-448-45252-4                    10 9 8 7 6 5 4 3 2

# PENGUIN YOUNG READERS

LEVEL 2

PROGRESSING READER

# We Love You,
## Strawberry Shortcake!

**by Sierra Harimann**
**illustrated by Marci Beighley**

Penguin Young Readers
An Imprint of Penguin Group (USA) Inc.

Strawberry Shortcake

is a berry sweet girl.

She likes to show
her friends how much
she cares about them.

Strawberry's friends like
to show they care, too.

Plum Pudding has an idea.

Everyone can give

Strawberry a gift.

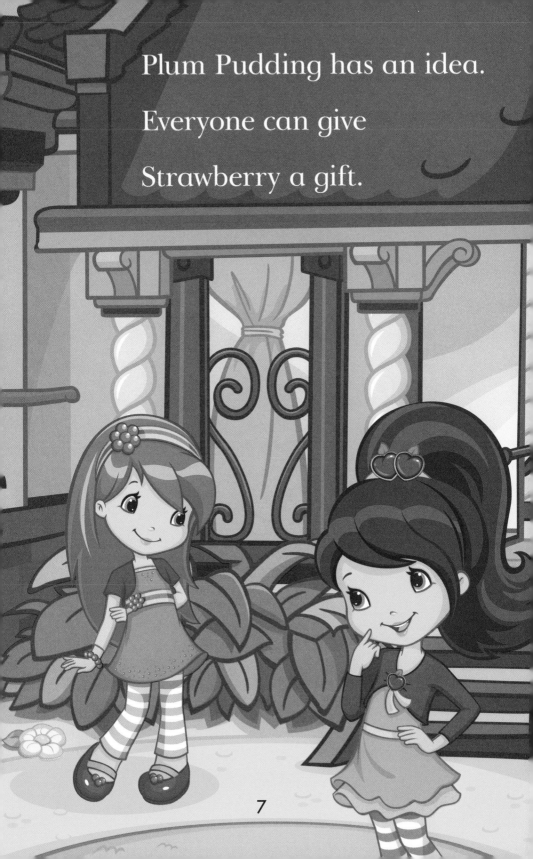

Raspberry Torte wants to throw

Strawberry a surprise party.

Both ideas are good.
The girls will have a party
**and** bring gifts!

Plum and Raspberry
know what to give Strawberry.
So do Lemon Meringue
and Blueberry Muffin.

Orange Blossom does not
know what to give Strawberry.
But then she gets an idea!

Strawberry's friends
set up for the party.
It will be berry fun!

It is almost party time.

Blueberry calls Strawberry.

She asks Strawberry

to come to the bookstore.

Strawberry says she will

come right away.

Strawberry opens the door.

What a surprise!

Lemon pours lemonade.

Raspberry serves fruit salad.

Plum is the first to give

Strawberry a gift.

It is a dance lesson!

Next, Blueberry
gives her gift
to Strawberry.

It is a book for

Strawberry's recipes.

Then, Lemon gives

her gift to Strawberry.

It is a haircut.

Next, Strawberry opens
a box from Raspberry.
Inside is a pretty,
new dress!

Orange feels very sad.

Her gift is not

like the other gifts.

Orange tells Strawberry
her gift was just
going to be a hug.

Strawberry thinks a hug

is a perfect gift!

Strawberry says,
"Thank you."
She loves her party
and all her gifts.

But Strawberry loves
her berry best friends
even more!